www.BillieBBrownBooks.com

First American Edition 2021
Kane Miller, A Division of EDC Publishing
Original Title: Billie B Brown: *The Hat Parade*

First published in Australia by Hardie Grant Egmont

For information contact:
Kane Miller, A Division of EDC Publishing
P.O. Box 470663
Tulsa, OK 74147-0663
www.kanemiller.com
www.usbornebooksandmore.com

Library of Congress Control Number: 2020937645

Printed and bound in the United States of America
1 2 3 4 5 6 7 8 9 10

ISBN: 978-1-68464-220-5

The Hat Parade

By Sally Rippin

Illustrated by Aki Fukuoka

Chapter One

Billie B. Brown has one shoebox, five feathers and three rolls of ribbon.

Can you guess what the "B" in Billie B. Brown stands for?

Box.

Jack is Billie's best friend. He lives next door. Today Jack is helping Billie make funny hats from boxes.

"Look at me!" Billie laughs. She puts a shoebox on her head. It is covered with feathers and ribbons.

Five feathers
One shoebox
Three rolls of ribbon

"That is the best
hat ever!" Jack laughs.
"You will definitely
win with *that* hat!"

Billie smiles. On Monday
there will be a
hat parade at school.
Billie **really**, **really**
wants to win the
prize for Best Hat.

Lola won last year.

This year Billie

is sure she can win!

"You should go in

the parade too, Jack!"

Billie says. She plops a

funny hat on his head

and giggles.

"Nah," says Jack.

His cheeks turn pink.

Billie knows he's too shy

to wear a fancy hat.

He is scared

the other kids

might laugh

at him.

Some boys

wear hats in

the parade. But usually

they wear plain old caps.

Or maybe they stick a

leaf in their school hats.

None of them wear

fancy hats. Billie thinks

they are silly. Fancy hats

are obviously the best.

Nobody has ever won

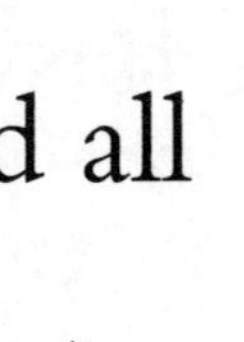

Best Hat in a cap!

Billie and Jack spend all

afternoon making hats.

Some of them are very funny! Billie's mom and dad invite Jack to stay for dinner. Everyone wears Billie's fancy hats to the table. They talk in funny voices. Baby Noah laughs so hard he spits mashed potato everywhere.

It has been the best day ever.

Chapter Two

The next day is Sunday. It rains all day. It rains so hard that Billie can't go outside to play. She tries to play with Noah, but he is too annoying. Billie gets mad at him.

Then Noah begins to cry. "Mom!" Billie yells. "Noah is messing up my game!"

"He is only little," Billie's mom says. "And he is feeling **cranky** because he has a cold." She takes Noah to have his nap.

Now Billie is *really* bored. She doesn't want to do any more crafts. And Dad says, "No more screens." Billie *really* wants to go outside and play.

She is so **wriggly** it feels like she has ants in her pants.

That afternoon, the rain begins to clear.

"Dad, look!" Billie shouts. "*Now* can I go outside?"

"All right," Dad says. "But put on your coat and hat. It's cold and wet outside."

"**Yay!**" Billie says.

She runs outside to find Jack. But she has forgotten something very important. Something her dad told her to do.

Can you remember what it is?

Billie and Jack ride their bikes up and down the lane. The wind **whooshes** through their clothes. It feels good to be outside after being stuck inside all morning.

"Look at me!" Billie

yells. She rides through a deep puddle. The muddy water splashes all around her. Now she is spattered with brown spots.

Soon it starts to rain again.
At first it rains lightly.
Then it rains harder.

"I'm going inside now,"
Jack says. "I don't want
to get wet."

"**It's only water!**"
Billie yells.

But by the time she goes
back inside she is as wet
and muddy as a puppy.

That night at the dinner table, Billie starts to **sneeze**. Her eyes water and her nose feels stuffy. Even though Billie's dad has cooked her **very** favorite dinner, Billie doesn't feel hungry at all.

Billie's dad tucks her into bed. Billie's face feels hot. Her head has begun to hurt.

"Hmmm ..." her dad says.

"It looks like you have caught a cold, Billie. You might have to stay home from school tomorrow."

"I can't stay home tomorrow," Billie says. "It's the hat parade!"

"Well, let's see how you feel when you wake up," her dad says.

He gives her some medicine for her headache. Then he tucks her into bed and kisses her good night.

Chapter Three

The next morning, Billie's whole body hurts. Her throat is sore, too. Outside the rain is pouring down.

Billie B. Brown is **sick**, **sick**, **sick**.

Jack comes to visit Billie before school. "I'm going to miss the hat parade," Billie croaks. She looks at all her beautiful hats sitting on her cupboard. She has spent so much time making them.

Now no one will see her hats. She feels a hot tear trickle down her cheek.

"Oh, Billie," says Jack. He looks sad. He puts the fanciest hat on his head. Then he makes a funny face to make his best friend laugh.

But it is no use. Billie feels sadder than ever.

"But you *have* to be in the parade," Jack says. "This is the best, most fancy hat ever!"

Billie hangs her head. "I guess Lola will win Best Hat again this year," she says, sighing.

Jack frowns and his cheeks turn very pink. "No," he says. "I will wear your hat in the parade, Billie. I'll win the prize for *both* of us!"

Billie stares at Jack in surprise. “But what if the other kids laugh at you?” she says.

“Who cares?” Jack says.

He looks in the mirror and shrugs. "It's good to make people laugh. Laughing is the best!"

Billie **giggles**. It is true. Laughing *does* make you feel better!

Chapter Four

All day, Billie feels achy and tired. Her dad stays home from work and makes Billie a bed on the sofa. Noah is at childcare and Billie's mom is at work.

Billie's dad lets her watch *Finding Nemo* three times in a row. He brings her lemon in hot water and chicken soup on a tray.

Billie likes being home with her dad, but she is sad she is missing the hat parade. Plus, her head is sore and her nose won't stop running. Billie has been through a whole box of tissues! It's no fun being sick.

After lunch, Billie's dad works on his computer.

Billie snoozes on the sofa. It rains all day. Billie wakes up when she hears Jack's voice in the kitchen.

"**Billie! Billie!**"

he yells. He runs into the family room.

"**Shhh!**" says Billie's dad. "Billie is sleeping."

"No, I'm not," Billie says.

She has been waiting all day to see him.

"How was the parade?" she asks. "Did we win Best Hat?"

Jack sits down next to Billie. He shakes his head. "No. Lola won Best Hat again. Her hat had a whole city built on it!" He frowns. "I'm sure her mom and dad helped her."

Billie sighs. "Oh well," she says. She looks at her fancy hat in Jack's lap.

Jack gets a strange look on his face. "What's so funny?" Billie asks.

"Well, Lola *did* win the Best Hat award," says Jack.

"But we won something even better!" Jack pulls two silky red ribbons out of his pocket and hands one to Billie.

Billie **gasps**. "What's this?"

"When I put your fancy hat on, some of the kids laughed at me," Jack says.

"But then Ms. Walton saw I was wearing the hat you made because you were sick today. So she made up a special award just for us. She called it the Best Friend award."

Jack grins. "No one laughed at me after that."

"**Wow!**" Billie says.
"The Best Friend award!"
She smiles up at Jack.
"That's *much* better than a
silly old hat award."

"That's what I thought,
too," Jack says.

Billie looks down
at the beautiful silky
red ribbon. It's the first
award she has ever won.

She feels very proud. She pins the ribbon to her pajama top. Jack pins his ribbon on, too.

Just then the rain stops. The sun begins to peek out from behind the clouds.

"Dad, look!" Billie says. "There's a rainbow.

Please can we go outside to see it? I've been inside *all* day. And I'm feeling *much* better now!"

"Well, OK. Just for a little bit …" Billie's dad says.

"Thanks, Dad!" Billie says. She jumps up from the sofa.

"But this time don't
forget your coat,"
her dad calls after her.

"I won't!" Billie says.

"Or your hat!" her
dad jokes. He hands
Billie her fancy hat.

"I'd better take a hat,
too," Jack giggles. He
picks up a tissue box and
puts it on his head.

Billie and Jack sit on the back porch. They look up at the beautiful rainbow. Billie strokes her silky red ribbon. Then she looks at Jack in his silly hat and laughs. "Ms. Walton is right," she says. "You really are the best friend ever."

"And the fanciest!" Jack grins.